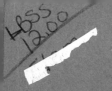

Sophie is only four years old, yet she knows exactly what she wants to be when she grows up—a lady farmer. She's saving up money to buy a cow, two hens, a pony, and a spotty pig, but in the meantime she makes do with flocks of insects and herds of snails. Sophie may be small but she's very determined. Everyone who knows her knows there's no doubt about that.

These charming and amusing stories by Dick King-Smith will delight young readers and the young at heart. That's because Sophie has a way with people—there's no doubt about that.

Sophie's
Snail

Sophie's Snail

by **Dick King-Smith**

Illustrated
by **Claire Minter-Kemp**

Delacorte Press

Published by Delacorte Press
Bantam Doubleday Dell Publishing Group, Inc.
666 Fifth Avenue, New York, New York 10103

This work was first published in Great Britain
by Walker Books Ltd.

Library of Congress Cataloging in Publication Data
King-Smith, Dick.
Sophie's snail / written by Dick King-Smith;
illustrated by Claire Minter-Kemp.
p.   cm.
Summary: Follows the humorous adventures of four-year-old
Sophie as she pursues her dream of becoming a farmer.
ISBN 0-385-29824-2
[1. Humorous stories.   2. England—Fiction.]
I. Minter-Kemp, Claire, ill.   II. Title.
PZ7.K5893So   1989   [Fic]—dc19
89-1098   CIP   AC

Manufactured in the United States of America
October 1989
10 9 8 7 6 5 4 3 2 1
BG

Contents

Sophie's
Snail

"What animal has got only one foot?" said their father.
"A chicken standing on one leg!" the twins said.

1

One Very
Small Foot

"What animal has got only one foot?" said the children's father. "I bet you can't tell me."

"I can!" said Matthew and Mark with one voice. As well as looking exactly alike, the twins nearly always said exactly the same thing at exactly the same time. Matthew was ten minutes older than Mark, but after that there had never been the slightest difference between them.

"Go on, then," said their father. "Tell me. What animal's got only one foot?"

"A chicken standing on one leg!" they said.

"That's silly," said Sophie seriously.

Sophie was four, a couple of years younger than her brothers.

"That's silly," she said. "It would still have a foot on the other leg. Anyway, Daddy, there isn't really an animal that's only got one foot, is there?"

"Yes, there is, Sophie."

"What?"

"A snail. Every snail has a big flat sticky muscle under it that it travels along on. That's called its foot. Next time you see a snail crawling along, pick it up carefully and turn it over, and you'll see. There are loads in the garden."

"Come on! Let's find one!" said Matthew to Mark and Mark to Matthew at the same time.

"Wait for me," said Sophie. But they didn't, so she plodded after them.

When she caught up with the twins, in a far corner of the garden, each was examining the underside of a large snail. Sophie was not surprised to see that the snails were also obviously twins, the same size, the same shape, the same striped greeny-browny color.

"I know!" said Matthew.

"I know what you're going to say!" said Mark.

"Let's have a snail race!" they said.

"How are you going to tell them apart?" said Sophie.

"I know!" said Mark.

"I know what you're going to say!" said Matthew.

"Fetch us a felt pen, Sophie," they said.

The twins had set their snails side by side on the path
that ran between the edge of the lawn and the flower bed.

"What are you going to do?" asked Sophie when she came back with a red felt pen.

"Put my initial on my snail," said Mark and Matthew together.

"But you've got the same initial."

The boys looked at each other.

"I know!" they said.

"I know what you're going to say," said Sophie, and she plodded off again. She came back with a blue felt pen.

After a moment, "Ready?" said Matthew, holding up his snail with a big red M on its shell, and at the same instant, "Ready?" said Mark, holding up his snail with a big blue M.

"Wait for me," said Sophie. "I haven't got a snail yet." But already the twins had set their twin snails side by side on the path that ran between the edge of the lawn and the flower bed. The path was made of big oval flagstones, and they chose the largest one, perhaps a meter long. The far end of the flagstone was to be the winning post.

"Ready, steady, go!" they shouted.

Sophie plodded off. "I'll beat them," she said. She was small but very determined.

Behind the first stone she moved, almost as though it had been waiting for her, was a snail. It was as different as possible from Red M and Blue M. It was very little, no

4

bigger than Sophie's middle fingernail, and it was a lovely buttercup yellow.

As she watched, it stretched out its head, poked out its two horns, and began to crawl, very slowly. It had a most intelligent face, Sophie thought. She picked it up carefully and turned it over.

"What a very small-sized shoe you would take, my dear," she said. "I don't know whether you can win a race, but you are very beautiful. You shall be my snail."

"Who won?" she said to Matthew and Mark when she returned.

"They didn't go the right way," they both said.

"But mine went farthest," they both said.

"No, it didn't," they both said.

They picked up their snails and put them side by side once more.

"Wait for me," Sophie said, and she put down the little yellow snail. It looked very small beside the others.

"Just look at Sophie's snail!" hooted the twins, but this time when they shouted "Ready, steady, go!" neither Red *M* nor Blue *M* would move. They stayed stubbornly inside their shells and took not the slightest notice of their owners' cries of encouragement.

Sophie's snail plodded off.

It was small but very determined, and Sophie lay on the

grass beside the path and watched it putting its best foot forward.

After half an hour it reached the winning post.

Sophie jumped up. "Mine's the winner!" she cried, but there was no one to hear. The twins had become bored with snail racing at exactly the same time and gone away. Red *M* and Blue *M* had gone away, too, into the forest of the flower bed. Only Sophie's snail kept stoutly on, while the straight silvery trail it had left glistened in the sunshine.

Sophie knelt down and carefully put her hand flat in front of the little yellow creature. It crawled solemnly onto it.

"You have such an intelligent look, my dear," said Sophie.

"What *have* you got in your hand, Sophie?" said her mother at teatime.

"It's Sophie's snail!" chorused Matthew and Mark.

"Put it straight out in the garden," said the children's mother.

"No," said Sophie in a small but determined voice.

Her mother looked at her, sighed, picked up a box of matches, emptied the matches out, and gave Sophie the empty box.

The snail crawled solemnly onto Sophie's hand.
"You have such an intelligent look, my dear," she said.

"Put it in there till after tea," she said, "and go and wash your hands."

All that evening Sophie played with her snail. When it was bedtime, and she was ready to wash and do her teeth, she put the snail carefully on the flat rim of the washbasin.

Then (as she always did) she filled the basin with warm water right up to the overflow and washed her face and hands. The snail did not move, though it appeared to be watching.

Then (as she always did) she brushed her teeth very hard, making a lot of froth in her mouth and spitting the bubbly blobs of toothpaste out on top of the rather dirty water. She always liked doing this. The toothpaste blobs made strange shapes on the surface of the water, often like a map of the world. Tonight there was a big white Africa at one side of the basin.

Then (as she always did) she pulled the plug out, but as she turned to dry her hands the sleeve of her dressing gown scuffed the rim of the basin. Right into the middle of disappearing Africa fell a small yellow shape, and then the last of the whirlpooling, frothing water disappeared down the drain, leaving the basin quite empty.

Sophie plodded down the stairs.

"My snail's gone down the drain," she said in a very quiet voice.

"You couldn't have kept it, you know," said her father gently. "It would have died anyway without its natural food."

"Next time you find one," said her mother, "just leave it in the garden. There are lots of other snails there, just as nice."

"Not as nice as my snail," said Sophie. She looked so unhappy that for once the twins said different things in an effort to comfort her.

" 'Spect it died quickly," said Matthew.

"Sure to be drowned by now," said Mark.

Try as she would, Sophie could not stop herself thinking about what happened to you if you went down a drain. She lay in bed and thought about the twins washing their hands in the basin and washing their teeth, and then later on Mum and Dad doing the same. All that water would be washing the body of her snail farther and farther away, down the drain into the sewer, down the sewer into the river, down the river into the sea.

When at last she slept she dreamed that she was walking by the seaside, and there she saw, washed up on the beach, a familiar little yellow shape. But when she ran and picked it up, it had no head, no horns, no foot. It was just an empty snail shell.

Sophie stared sadly into the
black depths of the drain.

Sophie woke early with the feeling that something awful had happened, and then she remembered what it was.

She plodded along to the bathroom and looked over the rim of the washbasin at the round drain with its metal grating, meant to stop things going down it

"But you were too small," she said.

Leaning over as far as she could reach, she stared sadly into the black depths of the drain. And as she stared, suddenly two little horns poked up through the grating, and then a head, and then a shell no bigger than her middle fingernail, a shell that was a lovely buttercup yellow.

Very carefully Sophie reached out and picked up her small determined snail.

Very quietly she plodded down the stairs and opened the back door and went out into the garden and crossed the dewy lawn.

Very gently, at the exact spot she had found it, she put her snail down and watched it slowly move away on its very small foot.

"Good-bye, my dear," said Sophie. "I hope we meet again." And then she sat happily on the wet grass watching, till at last there was nothing more to be seen of Sophie's snail.

"Well," said Sophie, "I'm going
to be a lady farmer. So there."

2

Farm Munny

"When I grow up," said Sophie at breakfast time, "I'm going to be a farmer."

"You can't," said the twins.

"Why not?"

"Farmers are men," they said.

"Well," said Sophie, "I'm going to be a lady farmer. So there."

Her father looked at her over the top of his newspaper.

"I'm sure you are, Sophie," he said. "I'm sure you could do anything you were determined to do. But you'd need an awful lot of money. Suppose you wanted to be a dairy farmer. Just think how much a big herd of cows would cost."

"I wouldn't have a big herd of cows," said Sophie.

"How many would you have?" asked Mark.

"I'd just have one cow, called Blossom."

"Well then, you wouldn't have much milk to sell," said her father.

13

"I wouldn't have any milk to sell," said Sophie.

"Why not?" asked Matthew.

"I should drink it all. I like milk."

She held out her glass.

"Can I have some more please, Mum?" she said.

"I don't really think," said her mother, "that you could call yourself a farmer . . ."

"A lady farmer," said the twins.

" . . . if the only thing you had was one cow."

"It wouldn't be the only thing," Sophie said. "I'd have two hens, called April and May."

"Why April?" said Matthew.

"Why May?" said Mark.

"Because they're nice months. And these would be nice hens."

"You wouldn't have many eggs to sell," said her father.

"I wouldn't have any eggs to sell," said Sophie.

"Because you'd eat them all," said Mark.

"Because you like eggs," said Matthew.

"I do," said Sophie. "I'm very fond of eggs."

She looked at the boiled egg that her mother had just put in front of her. Sophie had her own special blue egg cup with her name written on it in white letters. The egg was a big brown one.

"Excuse me, my dear," said Sophie, and she tapped it

14

Sophie tapped the egg gently with her spoon.
"I don't think it hurts them," she said.

gently with her spoon. "I don't think it hurts them," she said.

Matthew and Mark looked at each other, and each rolled his eyes upward and raised his eyebrows and tapped his forehead with one finger.

"What other animals will you keep?" said Sophie's father.

"A pony."

"What kind of pony?"

"A Shetland pony. I like Shetland ponies."

"But, Sophie," said her mother, "don't you think a Shetland pony will be rather small for you when you're a grown-up lady farmer? I mean, your legs will drag along the ground."

"I shan't ride it," said Sophie. "It'll just be a pet. I shall call it Shorty."

"What other pets will you keep?"

"Just a pig."

"Pigs aren't pets," said the twins.

"Measles will be."

"Why Measles?"

"Because he'll be a spotty pig, of course," said Sophie, looking scornfully at her brothers. "You've got no imagination, you two haven't."

She scraped the last bits out of her boiled egg and then

16

*"Measles will be a
spotty pig," said Sophie.*

turned it upside down on top of the egg cup so that it looked untouched.

"There you are, my dear," she said. "Good as new."

"Let me see if I've got it right," said her father. "When you're a lady farmer you're going to keep a cow and two hens and a pony and a pig. Am I right?"

"Yes," said Sophie. "And I shall grow a little field of corn."

"What for?" said Matthew and Mark.

"Cornflakes, of course," said Sophie. "Don't they teach you anything at school?"

"But what are you going to live on?" asked her father.

"Milk and eggs and cornflakes. I'm very fond of all those."

"No, no, I mean, how are you going to manage? None of the animals—Blossom and April and May and Shorty and Measles—is going to earn you any money. And how will you afford to buy them in the first place?"

"I shall save up."

"But that will take you years and years and years," said the twins.

"I've got years and years and years," said Sophie. With that she got down from the table and plodded off.

"She'll never get enough money to be a lady farmer," said Matthew.

"Will she, Dad?" asked Mark.

"I wouldn't be too sure about that," said their father. "Your sister may be small but she is a very determined person."

So nobody was very surprised next morning when Sophie came in to breakfast carrying her piggy bank and placed it on the table.

On its side was stuck a sign that said:

FARM MUNNY

THANK YOU

SOPHIE

Sophie's father put his hand in his pocket and took out a 20p piece and dropped it in. Her mother fetched her bag and added another.

Matthew and Mark looked at each other.

"I've only got two pennies," said Matthew.

"Same here," said Mark.

"Every little bit helps," said Sophie.

"Aunt Alice is coming to
see us," said their father.

3
Aunt Alice

The children's father looked up from the letter he was reading.

"It's from Aunt Alice," he said in rather a surprised voice. "She's coming to see us."

"Who's Aunt Alice?" asked the twins.

"She's Daddy's aunt," said their mother. "Or rather she's Grandpa's aunt, so she's Daddy's great-aunt."

"I've never seen a great-aunt," Sophie said.

"Well of course she's more than that to you three children. She's a great-great-aunt."

"Yikes!" said Sophie. "She must be *enormous!*"

"You'll soon be able to see," said her father. "She's asked herself to lunch next Sunday."

"Why haven't we seen her before?" asked Matthew and Mark.

"Because she lives about six hundred miles away, in the Highlands of Scotland."

"It's a long way to come for lunch," said Sophie.

"No, no, she's already down this way, staying in London for a few days."

The twins forgot almost at once about the coming visit of Great-Great-Aunt Alice, but Sophie didn't.

She wondered about the Highlands. How did you get down from them? On a rope? Or a ladder?

She wondered about this great-great-aunt. How would she get to London? In a train? But she might be too big to get through the train door. In an airplane perhaps? Yes, that would be best, in one of those huge ones with fat tummies that you could put tanks and trucks and things inside. The plane could fly off the top of the Highlands and then, when it got to London, they could open the big doors at the back and this enormous aunt could walk out.

But when Sunday came, and the front door opened, it was a very small person who walked in. The top of her head, Sophie could see, didn't even come up to Daddy's shoulder.

"Now then, Aunt Al," Sophie's father said, "these are the twins, Matthew and Mark."

"How de do?" said Aunt Alice, and she shook each boy's hand in turn.

"I'm four," said Sophie.
"How old are you?"

Although it wasn't always so, Matthew and Mark happened this day to be wearing exactly the same clothes.

"Like as two peas in a pod," said Aunt Alice. "Which is which?"

"I'm Matthew," said Matthew.

"I'm Mark," said Mark.

"I'm nearly ten minutes older," said Matthew.

"And I'm two years younger," said Sophie.

"Ah!" said Aunt Alice. "Now, you must be Sophie." She took hold of Sophie's hand and held it, looking at her with sharp blue eyes. She looked rather like a bird, Sophie thought, with those bright eyes and a thin beaky nose and hands that were skinny and bony and curled like a bird's claws.

"And how old are you, Sophie?" she said.

"I'm four," said Sophie. "How old are you?"

"Sophie!" said her mother. "You can't go asking things like that!"

"Why not?" said Sophie. "She asked me, didn't she?"

"Quite right," said Aunt Alice. "Load of rubbish, people not wanting to tell their age. I'm eighty. And I'm hungry as a hunter. When's lunch?"

After lunch Sophie and Aunt Alice sat on a swing seat on the lawn. Sophie's parents were doing the washing up and the

24

twins were playing with a soccer ball at the far end of the garden.

Aunt Alice's small shoes just touched the ground, and she swung the seat gently back and forth. Sophie sat beside her, feet sticking straight out, and looked directly at the bird face. I don't know about a great-great-aunt, she thought. Looks to me more like a small-small-aunt.

"What shall I call you?" she said.

"Same as everyone else does. Aunt Al. It's nice and short, like me."

"Are the Highlands very high, Aunt Al?" said Sophie.

"Quite high."

"And cold?"

"Quite cold."

"Lots of snow?"

"Masses, in winter."

"Polar bears?"

"No," said Aunt Alice. "But lots of lovely creatures, like golden eagles and blue hares and red deer."

They swung in silence for a while.

Then Sophie said, "It sounds nice. I wouldn't have bothered coming down off the top of the Highlands to go to London if I were you."

"I don't often. But there were a few things that I wanted to do."

25

"Like coming to lunch with us?"

"Of course. And doing some shopping. And seeing about my will."

"What's the matter with your Will?" said Sophie. "Is he ill?"

Aunt Alice gave a little chirp of amusement, but before she could answer, the twins came running up and stood side by side in front of her, grinning.

Sophie sighed.

She knew those identical grins.

She knew what was coming.

Still sighing, she wriggled down from the swing seat and plodded off.

Aunt Alice looked at the two boys.

"Hello," she said.

"Hello," they said.

"Guess . . ." said Matthew.

". . . which is which," said Mark.

"Bet you can't tell," they said.

It was a game they never tired of playing. If the visitor guessed wrong anyway, well and good. But if the guess was right, if the visitor pointed at Matthew and said "You're Matthew," he would reply "Mark"; and if Mark was correctly chosen, he would answer "Matthew." So they always won.

The twins stood side by side
in front of her, grinning.

Sophie did not approve of this.

"You tell lies," she said severely.

"No, we don't," they said. "We just say each other's name. That's not telling lies."

However, Sophie did not approve of telling tales either, so she had never said anything. Still, she would not watch when they played this game on people but always stumped off.

Aunt Alice looked at the grinning twins.

"Bet I can," she said.

She opened her bag and took out her purse. From it she took two pound coins.

"Tell you what," she said. "If I'm wrong, you each get one of these."

"All right!" they cried eagerly.

Aunt Alice stared long and carefully at each boy in turn, nodding her neat head up and down as if she were a thrush choosing between two worms. Then suddenly, like a bird pecking, she said, "Quick! Which of you's the older?" Before he could stop himself, Matthew twitched his mouth.

Aunt Alice looked at him poker-faced.

"You," she said deliberately, "are . . . Mark."

"No!" they both shouted delightedly. "No! You're wrong!"

28

"Honestly?" said Aunt Alice.

"Honestly," they said.

"In that case, I'd better pay up."

When Matthew and Mark had run off whooping and cheering, Sophie came plodding back. She climbed onto the swing seat.

"I've just been guessing which twin was which," Aunt Alice said.

"Huh!" said Sophie. She sighed.

"What ever can you mean?" said Aunt Alice.

Sophie looked very directly at her great-great-aunt.

"Aunt Al," she said. "Can you keep a secret?"

"Sure thing."

"Sometimes one of them pretends to be the other."

"Disgraceful," said Aunt Alice. "What wicked boys."

"I don't know," said Sophie. "They're all right really. They just get overexcited."

They sat side by side, swinging gently. For some time neither spoke. Each was comfortable with the silence.

Then Sophie said, "Did you give them money?"

"Yes."

"They'll only spend it."

"Wouldn't you, if I gave you money?"

"No, I'd save it. I'm saving up for a farm."

29

"Aunt Al," Sophie said.
"Can you keep a secret?"

"A toy one?"

"No, a real one."

"Whew! That'll take a long time."

"I expect it will," said Sophie.

Aunt Alice looked very directly at her great-great-niece.

"Sophie," she said. "Can you keep a secret?"

"Sure thing."

Aunt Alice took out her purse again.

"I gave the boys a pound coin each," she said, "but I'm going to give you two." And she did.

"Yikes!" said Sophie. "Thanks!"

"After all," said Aunt Alice with a grin, "it's not your fault that you're not twins."

When the twins found Sophie and asked her
to play soccer, she said she was too busy.

4

Dawn

"What shall we do this morning, Matthew?" said Mark.

"I know!" said Matthew.

"I know what you're going to say!" said Mark.

"Let's go and play soccer!" they said.

"Mum!" they shouted. "We're going out to play soccer."

"Well, take Sophie with you."

"She doesn't much like soccer."

"You never ask her. Go and ask her now." But when they found Sophie and asked her, she said she was too busy. So they went without her.

A little later Sophie's mother went out into the garden and found Sophie plodding around, peering into the flower beds as though searching for something. She was carrying a small yellow bucket.

"Why didn't you go with the twins?" her mother said.

"Too busy," grunted Sophie.

She bent down and picked up a used matchstick and put it in her bucket.

"Oh, you are a good girl, Sophie," said her mother, "picking up Daddy's old matchsticks. Every time he smokes his pipe he uses dozens of matches to keep the wretched thing alight, and then he chucks the used ones all over the garden. But wouldn't you rather be playing with the others than just picking up matchsticks?"

"I'm not just picking up matchsticks," said Sophie severely. "I'm collecting food for all of my animals."

Sophie's mother went back to her housework shaking her head. She's getting to be quite a loner, she thought. Collecting food for her animals indeed! Who ever heard of animals eating wood! She lives in a world of her own. It's not good for her. I wish there was a girl of her own age for her to play with.

A couple of weeks later Sophie's mother's wish was granted. A nearby house changed hands and the new people who moved in had a little girl who looked to be just about Sophie's age, a pretty little girl with golden hair done in ponytails.

Sophie's mother lost no time in making contact.

"Sophie," she said one morning, "those new people down the road have got a little girl."

"I know," said Sophie. "I've seen her. She wears dresses."

Sophie did not approve of dresses.

"She's called Dawn," said her mother.

34

*Sophie stumped off, shoulders hunched,
the very picture of disapproval.*

"Yuk," said Sophie. She thrust her hands into the pockets of her old jeans and stumped off, shoulders hunched, the very picture of disapproval.

"I've asked them to come by this morning," her mother called after her. She turned to the twins. "You three children can play with Dawn while we're having coffee," she said.

"What time are they coming?" said Matthew.

"Eleven o'clock."

"We've got a soccer match," said Mark.

"Kickoff half-past ten sharp," they said.

Dawn was wearing a green dress with bows on it, and short white socks, and smart red shoes. Her ponytails were tied with green ribbon. She carried a little toy pony.

Dawn's mother raised her eyebrows just a tiny bit as Sophie was called up to be introduced.

Sophie was wearing an old blue sweatshirt with her name written on it in white letters, and her old jeans, and her muddy boots. Her dark hair looked as though she had just come through a hedge backward. She carried her yellow bucket.

"Sophie," said her mother, "this is Dawn."

Dawn held out her toy pony. It was a bright pink pony with a long silvery mane and tail. It even had long silvery nylon eyelashes.

"This is Twinkletoes," she said. "He's my special favorite. But you can play with him if you like."

Dawn held out her toy pony.
"This is Twinkletoes," she said.

Sophie stared woodenly at Twinkletoes. It was plain from her expression that she did not approve of pink ponies.

"Yes, off you go and play," said Sophie's mother. "And, Sophie, you look after Dawn, there's a good girl."

Sophie stumped off with Dawn prancing beside her crying, "Gee-up, Twinkletoes! Gee-up, little pony!"

They came to the nearest flower bed, and Sophie began to hunt about.

"What are you looking for, Sophie?" asked Dawn.

"Matchsticks," said Sophie curtly. She found a couple and put them in her bucket.

"Ugh!" said Dawn, wrinkling her nose. "Nasty old matchsticks! Whatever d'you want them for?"

"To feed my animals on," said Sophie.

Dawn laughed. "You are silly, Sophie," she said. "Matchsticks are made of wood. Animals don't eat wood."

"Mine do," said Sophie.

"Isn't she silly, Twinkletoes?" said Dawn to her pony. "You wouldn't eat dirty old matchsticks, would you? You like nice grass." And she pulled some from the lawn and held them against the pink muzzle.

"You're just pretending to feed it," said Sophie scornfully. "My animals are real. I'll show you."

*　　*　　*

38

At the bottom of the garden was an old potting shed. Outside it, because they were too large to fit on the shelves, stood several very big flowerpots, upside down.

Carefully, Sophie tipped one of the big pots over. Underneath it, on a bed of used matchsticks, was a great army of wood lice.

"Good morning, my dears," said Sophie. "Here's two more nice juicy matchsticks for you."

"Ugh!" said Dawn, clasping Twinkletoes close to her. "Horrible dirty creepy-crawlies!"

At that moment a large wood louse detached itself from the mass and began to walk toward her feet.

Very deliberately, Dawn placed one of her smart red shoes on it and squashed it flat.

The yells from the bottom of the garden brought both mothers running. A dramatic scene met their eyes.

In front of the potting shed a small, stocky figure was jumping solemnly, up and down, boots together, on what had once been a bright pink pony with a silvery mane and tail but was now a dirty squashed lump.

"Sophie!" cried Sophie's mother.

"Dawn, darling!" cried Dawn's mother.

"Waaaaaaa!" cried Dawn.

The yells from the bottom of the garden brought both
mothers running. A dramatic scene met their eyes.

Sophie gave one final stamp on the battered body of Twinkletoes and plodded off.

"Where's Sophie?" asked the twins when they came back from their game.

"She's in her room. She's been extremely naughty."

"What did she do?"

"Never you mind."

"Where's Sophie?" asked her father when he came back from work.

"She's in her room. She's been extremely naughty."

"What did she do?"

"She completely ruined a toy belonging to the child of those new people down the road. Jumped on it. Squashed it."

"Why did she do that?"

"I don't know. I've asked her, but she won't answer."

"She'll answer me," Sophie's father said.

A few minutes later he came back.

"She won't," he said.

Even before Dawn's mother had said a frosty good-bye and taken her yelling daughter away, Sophie had gone straight to her room. She judged it better to go to her room

41

than to be sent there. She sat on the side of her bed, thinking sadly of the death of the wood louse. After a while the sad thoughts became glad ones. Dawn had paid for that! She would have to pay, too, out of her Farm Munny, but it would be worth it!

At bedtime the twins looked in on Sophie. They sat on the end of her bed, Matthew on one side and Mark on the other.

"What did you do?" they said.

"I busted Dawn's toy," said Sophie. "I jumped on it."

"Why?" said Mark.

"She squashed one of my wood louses," said Sophie.

"Squashed it dead?" said Matthew.

"Yes."

"What a beastly girl," they said.

"And the toy was a horrible pink pony called Twinkletoes."

"Yuk!" they said.

"You were right to jump on it," said Matthew.

"You should have jumped on her too," said Mark.

"Did you tell Mum and Dad what she did?" they asked.

"No," said Sophie. "They'd only say 'I'm sure she didn't mean to' or 'It was only a wood louse after all.' "

A little later Sophie's mother and father came in. They sat on the end of Sophie's bed, one on each side.

"You know, Sophie," said her father, "you simply can't go breaking other children's toys."

"I can," said Sophie. "I just have."

"You'll have to say you're sorry," said her mother.

"I can't," said Sophie. "I'm not."

"Look, Sophie," they said, "we know what Dawn did. The boys told us."

Sophie waited.

"I'm sure she didn't mean to," said her mother.

"It was only a wood louse," said her father, "after all."

Sophie was walking around the garden,
wearing a pair of her mother's sunglasses.

5

A Bad Back

Sophie was walking around the garden, wearing a pair of her mother's sunglasses. They were very dark glasses with a white frame. They made Sophie look like a panda. They made pink flowers look red and yellow flowers look golden and cabbages look blue.

Sophie walked along the path that ran along the front of the house and peered in through the dining-room window. Inside, everything looked very dark, the dining table, the chairs, the dresser with its rows of plates. The wood-block floor, usually the color of milk chocolate, had turned to plain. But whatever in the world was that long shadowy thing lying on the floor?

"Yikes!" shouted Sophie. "It's a dead body!" And she galloped off down the path and through the back door and into the kitchen.

"Mum!" she cried. "There's a dead body on the dining-room floor."

45

*In the dining room Sophie's father
lay flat on the hard wood-block floor.*

"A dead body?" said her mother, busy stirring something. "I hope not, Sophie. But you're right. There is a body on the dining-room floor."

"Whose?" said Sophie in a strangled voice.

Her mother turned from the stove.

"Goodness me!" she said. "You look like a panda. Take those things off. No wonder you couldn't recognize your own father."

In the dining room Sophie's father lay flat on the hard wood-block floor, his arms by his sides, and stared gloomily at the ceiling.

Sophie peeped around the door.

"Daddy?" she said.

"Yes."

"Are you all right?"

"No."

"What's the matter?"

"My back hurts."

"I'm not surprised," said Sophie. "Lying on that hard old floor. If you wanted to have a rest, why didn't you go to bed?"

Sophie's father sighed.

"It's not because I'm lying on the floor that my back hurts," he said. "It's because my back hurts that I'm lying on the floor."

47

"Oh," said Sophie. She walked across the room and stood, feet apart, hands on hips, staring down at her father's upturned face with a worried frown on her own. "What have you done to your back?" she said.

"I don't know," said her father in a grumpy voice. "All I did was bend down to pick up a newspaper and something went *click*."

"And it hurt?"

"It certainly did."

"Does it now?"

"It's okay as long as I keep still and flat like this. It's the best thing to do, they say, but it's pretty boring."

Sophie lay down beside her father, her arms by her sides, and stared thoughtfully at the ceiling.

"Would you like to play a game?" she said.

"Not if there's any moving about in it."

"No," said Sophie. "We can play I Spy. You'll only need to move your eyes. That won't hurt your back. Playing I Spy will take your mind off it."

"Oh, all right," said her father. "You start."

"I spy," said Sophie, "with my little eye, something beginning with . . . . *s*."

Sophie's father swiveled his eyes around the room. There was a row of saucers on the dresser.

"Saucer," he said.

48

"You can't see the seaside," said Sophie.
"Yes, I can, in that picture," said her father.

"No."

He looked at the hanging light.

"Shade," he said.

"No."

On the wall there were pictures.

"Seaside," he said.

"You mustn't cheat, Daddy," said Sophie severely. "You can't see the seaside. It's miles and miles away."

"Yes, I can, in that picture."

"Oh. No, it's not that."

"I give up."

"You can't," said Sophie. "You can't just give up. But I'll give you a hint if you like."

"Go on, then."

"Look above your head."

Sophie's father stared upward.

"All I can see is the ceiling," he said.

"I knew you'd get it," said Sophie, "if you kept trying."

"Actually, Sophie," said her father, *"ceiling* begins with a *c."*

"How silly of it," said Sophie. "Well, then it doesn't count. It's my turn again."

Half an hour later Sophie's mother came in.

"Oh, I see you're being looked after," she said. "Perhaps you'll be a nurse when you grow up, Sophie."

"You know I'm going to be a lady farmer. Go on, Daddy, it's your turn."

"What are you playing?" said her mother.

"We're playing I Spy," said Sophie. "I'm winning."

"I think you've won," said her father hollowly. "We've spied every single thing in the room. Why don't you run out in the garden now?"

"Oh, no," said Sophie. "It's much more fun playing with you. I know lots more games. I'll just go and get some things." And she plodded off.

Sophie's mother smiled.

"Poor old chap," she said. "You're a prisoner. You can't escape."

"I don't know how much more play I can stand," said Sophie's father.

"You'll just have to take it all lying down," said Sophie's mother. "The longer you can stay there, the better." And she went out just as Sophie returned with her arms full. She was carrying paper and pencils, a checkerboard and a box of checkers, a pack of cards, and a set of Happy Families.

"There!" said Sophie, dumping them all beside her father. "That'll do for a start."

"I can't play all those games," said her father desperately. "Not when I'm lying flat."

"You can hold things in your hands, can't you?" said Sophie.

51

"I suppose so."

"Right. Here's a pencil and paper, then. We'll begin with Tic-Tac-Toe."

At the end of a long, long morning, Sophie's mother came in again.

Sophie was sitting cross-legged beside her father. On her face was a look of triumph.

"Please, can I have Miss Bun the Baker's Daughter?" she said. "And Master Bones the Butcher's Son?"

She pointed at the one remaining card.

"You," she said, "must be Doctor Dose the Doctor."

Wearily her father handed over Doctor Dose. His face wore a look of great suffering.

"Is it your back?" Sophie's mother said. "Is it worse?"

Sophie's father moved his head from side to side on the floor.

"No," he said. "I haven't had time to think about it."

"We've had loads of games," Sophie said. "I won nearly all of them."

"Go and wash your hands for lunch, Sophie," her mother said, and, when Sophie had gone out, "How are you going to manage? Can you eat down there? The doctor should be here soon. Hadn't you better stay there till he comes?"

"I . . . am . . . not . . . staying . . . one . . . minute . . . longer," said Sophie's father.

"Hello," Sophie said.
"Is your name Dose?"

Very carefully, he levered himself to his feet.

Very gingerly, he took a couple of steps toward the door.

"It does feel better," he said in a tone of surprise.

"I told you so, Daddy," said Sophie, coming back. "I told you playing games would take your mind off it."

In the middle of lunch the doorbell rang. Sophie answered it. It was the doctor.

"Hello," she said. "Is your name Dose?"

"Dose?" said the doctor. "No, it's Macdonald."

"Oh," said Sophie. "Well, come in anyway."

"What's this I hear?" said the doctor, coming into the dining room. "Trouble in this happy family? Done your back in, have you?"

"It feels a lot better now," said Sophie's father.

"Does it?" said the doctor. "Well, I can tell you one thing for sure, before I even have a look at you. There's only one way to deal with a bad back."

"There is?" said Sophie's father.

"Yes. The moment you've finished lunch, you lie down flat on it, on this nice hard wooden floor, and you stay there the rest of the day."

He turned to Sophie.

"You'll keep Daddy company, won't you?" he said. "Perhaps you could think of some games to play."

54

*"There's only one way to deal
with a bad back," said the doctor.*

One of the Bad Things about Going to School
would be having to wear a School Uniform.

6

Such an Intelligent Look

It was September and the twins had just gone back to school. Next term Sophie would be going too. She thought about this and wondered if she would like it. There would be Good Things and Bad Things about Going to School.

The Bad Things would be:

1. Having to wear a School Uniform.
2. Having to meet Dawn again, for Dawn was starting this very term.
3. Having to meet other Strange Children, as awful as Dawn.
4. Having to meet strange Grown-ups; the Teachers might be awful, too; Matthew and Mark said that they weren't, but you could never tell.
5. Having to eat School Lunches, especially sardines in tomato sauce.

Sophie fancied throwing
someone down—Dawn perhaps.

Of course there would be Good Things, too, thought Sophie.

1. Not having to help wash up the breakfast things at home.
2. Being with her brothers in school. She did not know that once she was at school they would not take the slightest notice of her.
3. Drinking Morning Milk: At home Mum always said, "If you're thirsty, have a drink of water—milk's fattening," but Sophie knew at school you were encouraged to drink your Morning Milk and sometimes there were extra bottles if children were away.
4. Doing Judo: Sophie fancied throwing someone down—Dawn perhaps.
5. Farming Lessons: You went to school, Sophie knew, to be taught things, for when you were grown-up. They would say "What are you going to be?" and she'd say "A lady farmer," and then they'd give her Farming Lessons.

Sophie's present farming was carried out in the potting shed. Here she kept her flocks and herds.

She had a new system of free-range wood-louse farming. She had given up collecting matchsticks, which they didn't much seem to like, and now kept the wood lice in a seed tray so that they could come and go as they pleased, and she fed them on cornflakes. The cornflakes seemed to disappear, though she had never actually seen a wood louse chewing one.

This morning there were only three wood lice in the seed tray, and one of those was lying upside down, its seven pairs of legs pointed at the roof of the potting shed.

"I hope *you* haven't hurt your back, my dear," said Sophie, grinning as she tipped it the right way up. She dropped a couple of cornflakes into the tray.

"I wonder where the rest of the herd has got to?" she said.

On a country holiday Sophie had once seen a farmer calling in his dairy herd for milking. "Cow! Cow! Cow!" he had shouted, and the big black-and-white animals had all started walking across the field toward him.

"Louse! Louse! Louse!" Sophie shouted, but nobody came, so she ate the rest of the handful of cornflakes. She went on to inspect the rest of her stock in their various pens on an old table in the shed.

First there was a shoe box. On it was written SENTIPEEDS. There were two in it, one large and dark, one small and brown. Sophie was planning to increase the size of this flock, but wild centipedes were difficult animals to capture, so quickly did they scuttle. She was not sure what they ate and was trying them with cookie crumbs.

*There were two centipedes in it, one
large and dark, one small and brown.*

"These shouldn't upset you, my dears," she said. "They're digestives."

Next, there was an old cake tin full of soil and earthworms. Earthworms ate earth, Sophie knew, so there were no feeding problems here. She was only really interested in the largest worms and measured her captures with an old wooden ruler. This was difficult, because it takes two people to stretch out a wriggling worm and she needed Matthew or Mark to hold one end. Her record to date was a giant of fifteen centimeters.

Beyond the worm can was another shoe box marked YEAR WIGS. Earwig-keeping was a branch of Sophie's farming that she had only recently taken up, thanks to her great-great-aunt. Before Aunt Al's visit Sophie had been wary of these dangerous-looking beasts with their crescent-shaped nippers.

"They bite," she had said.

"Load of rubbish," Aunt Al had said. "No good being scared of animals if you're going to be a farmer. Go and catch one and bring it here." And Sophie had caught one (cautiously, using an empty matchbox as a trap) and Aunt Al had picked it out and it hadn't bitten her.

"You have to be firm with them," she had said. "Don't stand any nonsense."

So now Sophie collected earwigs (still using the matchbox) and fed them on fruit. She dropped a rotten plum into the box before moving on to a coffee jar on whose glass wall hung a single enormous slug. It was dark brown, with a lovely orange rim around its huge sticky foot. Sophie put a bit of cabbage leaf into the jar. She was quite proud of this monster, whose capture had covered her hands in a thick slime that took pumice stone to get off.

But her favorite animals were in the last pen of all, a large cardboard box, and she opened the lid of this and tore up the rest of the cabbage leaf and dropped it in. Under the black printed lettering on the side of the box (which said BAKED BEANS) was a single word in big red capital letters (which said SNALES).

Ever since the day of the Great Snail Race, Sophie had become especially fond of these creatures. She would spend ages watching them crawl along in their dignified way, wiggling their stalky eyes and leaving glistening silvery trails on the potting-shed table.

Every day Sophie would go on a snail hunt around the garden, adding to her herd, and there were seldom less than twenty in the box, of all shapes and sizes and shades of green or brown. The number varied because Sophie had cut a lot of snail-sized holes in the lid of the large box so that anyone who wished could leave.

But always in the back of Sophie's mind—as she turned over stones or peered into cracks in the garden wall or searched in the flower beds—was the hope that

Every day Sophie would go on a snail hunt
around the garden, adding to her herd.

one day, perhaps, she just might meet again one very particular snail.

"What did you have for lunch?" Sophie asked the twins when they came home from school.

"Sardines in tomato sauce," they said.

Sophie's face fell.

"Did you see Dawn?" she said.

"Yes," said Matthew. "She's got a new pony."

"A blue one," said Mark.

"Were there lots of Strange Children?"

"Lots."

"Very strange."

Sophie tried a couple of Good Things.

"Did you do Judo?" she said.

"Only juniors do Judo," they said.

"Well, did you have Farming Lessons?"

Matthew and Mark looked at each other, and each rolled his eyes upward and raised his eyebrows and tapped his forehead with one finger.

Gloomily, Sophie stumped off.

But after that the day improved.

First, she found a large earwig and actually caught it with her bare hands. Then she found a very pretty caterpillar, which she put into a small box in the potting shed. She

The snail stopped and raised its head in greeting.
"Good evening, my dear," Sophie said softly.

was not too sure how to spell it, so she simply wrote CAT on the box.

Good luck comes in threes, thought Sophie that evening as she gazed out her bedroom window. It was a beautiful September evening. No one could possibly have been unhappy on such an evening, not even faced with sardines in tomato sauce.

Sophie leaned on the sill and played with a little tendril that was trying to creep across it unnoticed. She looked straight down the creeper-covered wall and there, right under her nose and climbing up toward it, was a very small snail, a snail no bigger than Sophie's middle fingernail, a snail that was a lovely buttercup yellow.

Very slowly (but very determinedly) it plodded up the last few inches of wall and over the edge of the windowsill. Then it stopped and raised its head in greeting. It had such an intelligent look.

Sophie's face lit up in one enormous grin.

"Good evening, my dear," she said softly. "What took you so long?"

About the Author

Dick King-Smith is the author of many popular books for children, including HARRY'S MAD and THE SHEEP-PIG, winner in England of the *Guardian* Award for Children's Fiction. In the United States, under the name BABE, THE GALLANT PIG, it was named an American Library Association Notable Book. Mr. King-Smith's most recent book for Delacorte Press was THE FOX BUSTERS. He lives in a seventeenth-century cottage in England with his wife.